Series by Tevin Hansen:

Hairytale Adventures:

Alexia & Melvin: The Birthday Bear

Alexia & Melvin: The Museum Guide

Alexia & Melvin: The Zookeeper

Junkyard Adventures:

Word Dragon

Sea Serpent of Science

Giant of Geography

Alien of Astronomy

Art Monster

Halloween Adventures:

The Halloween Grump

The Haunted Hospital

The Space Adventure

Handersen Publishing, LLC
Lincoln, Nebraska

Hairytale Adventures Book 1
Alexia & Melvin
The Birthday Bear

Text copyright © 2020 Tevin Hansen
Interior Illustration copyright © 2020 Tevin Hansen
Cover copyright © 2020 Handersen Publishing, LLC
Cover Art by Shaun Cochran
Interior Design by Nichole Hansen
Manufactured in the United States of America.

Library of Congress Cataloging-in-Publication Data

Names: Hansen, Tevin, author, illustrator.
Title: Alexia & Melvin: The Birthday Bear / Tevin L Hansen.
Description: Lincoln, Nebraska : Handersen Publishing, LLC, 2019. | Series: Hairytale Adventures ; book 1 | Audience: Ages 6-9. | Audience: Grades 2-3. |
    Summary: Smart girl Alexia must team up with bully Melvin when only she can see that the entertainer at his birthday party is an imposter--a very hungry one.
Identifiers: LCCN 2019030865 (print) | LCCN 2019030866 (ebook) | ISBN 9781947854888 (paperback) | ISBN 9781947854895 (hardback) | ISBN 9781947854901 (ebook)
Subjects: CYAC: Bears--Fiction. | Birthdays--Fiction. | Parties--Fiction. | Bullying--Fiction.
Classification: LCC PZ7.1.H36433 Bir 2019 (print) | LCC PZ7.1.H36433 (ebook) | DDC [Fic]--dc23
LC record available at https://lccn.loc.gov/2019030865
LC ebook record available at https://lccn.loc.gov/2019030866

Publisher Website: www.handersenpublishing.com
Publisher Email: editors@handersenpublishing.com
Author Website: www.tevinhansen.com
Cover Artist Website: www.shaunyredcomet.com

Hairytale
Adventures
1

The Birthday Bear

Tevin Hansen

Handersen Publishing, LLC
Lincoln, Nebraska

Helpful List

1. Chewed Up Like Cheese & Crackers

2. Melvin McNatt & the Wiggly Worm

3. Bee Stings & Handshakes

4. Why I Spent My Allowance on a Bully

5. The Special Guest

6. Adults Taste Like Smelly Old Socks

7. The Adults Get Tricked

8. The Most Amazing Trick of All

9. Caught by the Birthday Bear

10. Don't Tell Lies

11. Free Money

12. Battle of the Brains

13. The Biggest Splash Contest

14. P.S.

This is **NOT** a nice story.

There is a tricky, nasty, hungry bear in this story. And kids being mean. And lots of other bad stuff too.

But there is also bravery.

And kindness.

And friendship.

Please take this book seriously.

It could save your life.

Your friends,

Alexia & Melvin.

Chapter 1

Chewed Up Like Cheese & Crackers

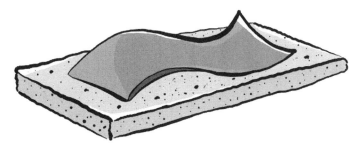

My name is Alexia. But all it took was one kid at school to call me "Alex," and then everyone made fun of me.

"Alex is a *boy's* name," said Katrina Belcher, a mean girl in my class. She and her friends found me reading during recess.

When I explained to them that Alex was an androgynous name that could be used by either a boy or a girl, they got confused.

"An-drogy-*what*?" they said.

Those girls had no idea what I was talking about, so they made up a song about me.

"Alexia, Alexia, she has dyslexia…" they sang. "Alexia, Alexia, she's so dumb."

"That doesn't even rhyme," I told them. "And even if I did have dyslexia, I would still be smarter than all of you. Dyslexia doesn't have anything to do with how smart you are. It has to do with processing letters and sounds. Lots of kids with dyslexia grow up and do amazing things, like become scientists, teachers, professors, and authors. Which is more than any of you will ever grow up to be."

They just stared at me.

"Don't listen to her," said Katrina, who was probably the meanest girl in the whole entire school. "Alexia is dumb. She's dumber than the whole world."

"I'm not dumb," I told her. "Miss Mandy said that I'm the smartest student she's ever had. She told me that I'm probably smarter than the rest of the class put together."

"What-*ever*," said Katrina. Then she and her friends went to go bug somebody else.

I love saying stuff like that. Mostly because it makes them really mad. After that, they usually leave me alone.

I may be a kid, but I know things.

Lots of things.

I wasn't lying when I told those girls about what Miss Mandy said to me last week. I can't help it if I'm smarter than most kids.

I just am.

Not only am I smart, I can also spot things that other kids usually miss. One important thing I've learned is how to spot an **IMPOSTER**.

I can easily tell when someone isn't who they say they are.

For example—

Two weeks ago, we had a substitute teacher. A man walked into our classroom that I immediately recognized. He had a white beard and twinkly blue eyes. He was the man who pretended to be Santa Claus at the mall last Christmas. I knew it was him right away, but the rest of the class had no idea that this man was an **IMPOSTER**. He was a *real* teacher, but not the *real* Santa.

And it's a good thing I can spot these types of **IMPOSTERS**. Otherwise those nine kids from my school would have been chewed up like cheese and crackers by that nasty old bear.

Chapter 2

Melvin McNatt & the Wiggly Worm

Melvin McNatt goes to my school. He's in the same grade as me, and the same class. Melvin is not a nice person.

Melvin is a bully.

All of his friends are bullies too.

Yesterday at school, Melvin tried to make me eat a worm. Not a small worm, but a large, disgusting, wiggly worm. He and his friends cornered me outside the school library.

"Go ahead, smarty-pants," Melvin said to me. He dangled the worm right in my face. "Eat the worm, Alexia. It's good for you."

"You're probably right, Melvin," I told him. "Worms are full of protein. And did you know that worms are considered a delicious treat in some countries? We should all enjoy a healthy worm diet. How about worm soufflé? Or maybe hummus made with worms? Or maybe a nice big bowl of Baba ghanoush with worms?"

"Baba-what? Baba-who?" Melvin said with a confused look on his face. His friends all laughed at him because he couldn't come up with a smart reply. Instead of making me eat the worm, Melvin threw it at me.

I am not afraid of worms.

But I am afraid of great big bears.

And you should be too.

Chapter 3

Bee Stings &
Handshakes

Two weeks ago, my dad pretty much saved Melvin's life. My dad was driving home from work when he spotted Melvin coughing and choking on the side of the road.

Melvin had discovered a bees' nest hanging from a tree. He threw rocks at it, thinking nothing would happen.

Well, something *did* happen.

One big rock hit the bees' nest, then the nest fell from the tree and landed at Melvin's feet. He thought this was quite funny, so he began to hit the nest with a stick to break it open. The buzzing grew louder and louder.

Smack, smack, smack!

Melvin hit the bees' nest with his stick, over and over, until he destroyed their home.

The bees did not like this.

"Ouch!" Melvin cried. "Ouch! OUCH!"

Melvin felt a few quick stabs on his arms. Then his chest, legs, and on his back. There was one bee sting for each of his ears. He also received one sting near his throat.

And *that* was the bee sting that got Melvin into serious trouble.

It was a good thing my dad happened to be driving by that day. My dad waved at Melvin, recognizing him from the neighborhood.

Melvin waved back, but not because he was being polite. (Melvin doesn't know *how* to be polite.) It was because he was having trouble breathing.

Melvin is allergic to wasp and bee stings.

About an hour later, my dad called the McNatts from the hospital and told them what happened.

Melvin's parents raced down to the hospital, each one of them driving a luxury car. The McNatts are both doctors, so they could afford stuff like that.

"Oh, my poor baby!" cried Mrs. McNatt the moment she entered Melvin's hospital room. "My poor honey bear!"

The doctor explained that Melvin was severely allergic to wasp and bee stings.

"He should have been tested years ago," the doctor told them. "Your son is lucky to be alive."

The McNatts looked very guilty. They are both very smart doctors, but neither one of them had any idea that their son was super allergic to bee stings.

Or that he's a bully.

Or that he has rocks in his head.

The McNatts think their son is a wonderful, kind young man with excellent manners.

The McNatts were very grateful to my dad for saving their son.

"You saved my son's life," Mr. McNatt said as he shook my father's hand. "I owe you one, I guess. Let me know if you ever need anything. Maybe some insoles with extra arch support, or a foot massage…"

That's how my dad and Melvin's dad

became friends. And that's also why I was invited to Melvin's birthday party on Saturday.

A day that would turn out to be the worst day of my whole entire life.

For me *and* Melvin.

Chapter 4

Why I Spent My Allowance on a Bully

Melvin's birthday party started at noon. When I looked at the clock, I saw that it was already 11:45 a.m. I was still in my bedroom, deciding what to wear.

My dad hollered up the stairs. "Ready to go, Alexia? Almost time for the party!"

My dad was all set to walk me over to the McNatts house, which is the biggest house in the whole neighborhood. Their place has huge front windows, tall hedges, and a great long driveway that goes in a loop.

"Yes, I'm ready," I said, coming downstairs. I was wearing my favorite pair of jeans and a brand-new purple T-shirt. My mom wanted me to wear a dress to the party, but I disagreed. To make her happy, I let her comb my hair and tie in some purple ribbons.

From our house to the McNatts house was not very far. But it felt like a long way because I was carrying Melvin's birthday gift.

I bought him a basketball.

Even though I didn't want to spend any of my allowance money on a school bully, I did. Mostly I did it because I knew he'd be getting some really nice presents from the other kids. And I didn't want to be pointed out, or made fun of by Melvin and his friends.

I get enough of that at school.

I thought that if Melvin had something fun to play with at school (like a basketball), there would be no time for him to bother me or try and make me eat worms. I also thought that because I bought such an expensive gift, this entitled me to eat as much birthday cake and ice cream as I wanted.

My dad and I stood at the McNatts front door. I got to push the fancy doorbell.

Bzzzzzzt!

Melvin answered the door wearing a brown suit with a red bow tie. He did not look happy. I took one look at him and tried hard not to laugh.

"Hello, Alexia," Melvin said. "I am so glad you could make it. You look very nice today."

This didn't sound much like the Melvin I knew from school. That Melvin always sounded rude. This Melvin sounded more like a robot that had memorized the lines his mother had taught him.

Mrs. McNatt was standing behind her son. She wore a pretty red dress with flowers on it. She was tall and thin, with a perfect smile that showed off her dazzling white teeth.

Mrs. McNatt is a dentist. She's the one who smiles at you and says "this won't hurt a bit!" right before she starts drilling into your teeth, making you jump out of the chair. I suppose she wanted to be sure that her son greeted the guests politely.

"Thank you for coming to my party, Alexia," Melvin said in his robot voice. "I hope you have a wonderful time. We will play games, eat birthday cake, and have lots of fun. Won't you please come in?"

"Sure," I said. "Why not."

Chapter 5

The Special Guest

My dad left me at the front door.

"Have a great time, Alexia!" he told me as he headed back home. "I'll be back to pick you up in a few hours."

I waved goodbye to my dad and went inside. Melvin and Mrs. McNatt led me through the house, which was full of fancy paintings and weird sculptures. Our house was mostly filled with library books and half-finished art projects.

We went through the kitchen, out onto the deck, then into the huge backyard. The backyard was set up for a wonderful party. There was music playing, decorations and balloons everywhere, and confetti all over the place. In the middle of the yard was a long table piled high with presents and food. There was even a big banner hanging up.

Happy Birthday!
To Our Little Pookie Bear

I was the last guest to arrive. So now everyone was angry at me because Mrs. McNatt told them they would have to wait until *all* the guests had arrived before they could eat.

"So glad you could make it, Alexia!" said Mr. McNatt as he waved me over to the picnic table. I was surprised by how happy he seemed. Especially considering he's a podiatrist—a foot doctor. He gets paid lots of money to touch other people's sore, swollen, smelly feet. You'd have to pay *me* lots of money to touch other people's feet too. He and his smiley wife seemed to be the only ones who were glad that I came to the party.

"Sit anywhere you like, Alexia," said Mr. McNatt. "We couldn't begin without you. So now that you're here, we can get this party started!"

There were thirteen people in total at the party. Mr. and Mrs. McNatt, the nanny, me and Melvin, plus eight other kids I recognized from school.

Everyone wore a pointy red birthday hat, including the adults. Mr. McNatt handed me a hat too, and I put it on. Then I took my seat at the far end of the table.

"Finally, we can eat," said Katrina Belcher. "I'm as hungry as a bear."

A few kids pointed at me and started to whisper. Then they sang their dumb song.

"Alexia, Alexia, she has dyslexia…"

I heard another one of Melvin's friends say, "Why was *she* invited anyway?"

I ignored them and stared at all the food. The table was loaded with all sorts of yummy foods, tasty sweets, and cold drinks. Everything looked so good that I didn't know where to begin.

I wanted a scoop, slice, or piece of everything on the table. I would try them all, and taste every treat that I possibly could.

"Let's eat!" Mr. McNatt said, and all the other kids did exactly that.

After I loaded up my plate, I placed a napkin on my lap, and picked up my fork. But just as I was about to take my first bite…

"Everyone look!" Mrs. McNatt cheered. "The special guest has just arrived!"

My stomach turned into a big twisted knot when I saw what came walking through the side gate. When everyone turned to look, they all clapped and cheered for the special guest.

I didn't cheer.

I suddenly got very scared.

The special guest was an **IMPOSTER**.

Chapter 6

Adults Taste Like Smelly Old Socks

The **IMPOSTER** was big, brown, hairy, and really tall. He was dressed up like a clown. He wore a big red nose to cover his long snout, and silly glasses to disguise his cold brown eyes. He also wore a pointy hat like all the other guests, but there were words printed on his party hat.

The Birthday Bear

31

"Where's the special birthday boy?" the Birthday Bear asked, grinning with a mouth full of sharp teeth. "I heard that somebody is turning another year older today!"

Melvin raised his hand.

The Birthday Bear went over to him and acted silly. He talked and made jokes while he tied balloons around Melvin's ears.

Melvin's face turned red, but it was all in good fun. The kids and grownups thought the bear was really funny.

Not me.

I saw right through his lame jokes and funny talk. I knew he was a real bear that wanted to eat us for lunch. The bear didn't want to eat the adults, only the children.

Everyone knows that bears think that adults taste like vinegar and smelly old socks. But to a bear, kids taste even more delicious than a big slice of birthday cake.

"Looks like I'm just in time for lunch," the Birthday Bear said. "Dig in, everyone! I can perform my magic show after everyone has filled their tummy."

The Birthday Bear talked and made more jokes while everyone ate lunch.

"What about you, Mr. Bear?" Melvin asked with his mouth full. "Aren't you hungry?"

"Oh, I'm real hungry," the Birthday Bear said, which sent a shiver down my back. "But I never eat before a performance. Even though I've been doing this for a long time, sometimes I still get nervous."

I couldn't believe that I was the only one who noticed that the Birthday Bear's costume had no zipper. That's because it was the *real* fur of a *real* bear. And nobody seemed to understand this.

I kept a close watch on him during lunch. I knew that the bear was hungry, but I guess he didn't want to spoil his appetite. If they could, bears would gobble up kids for breakfast, lunch, and dinner.

People eat fish 'n' chips.

Bears eat fish 'n' kids.

Chapter 7

The Adults Get Tricked

After lunch, the Birthday Bear put on a show for us. I have to admit that it was an excellent show. The Birthday Bear did all sorts of magic tricks, made jokes, and kept everyone laughing.

It was all very entertaining.

During his performance, I had nearly forgotten that he was an **IMPOSTER**.

I wanted to warn everyone, but I didn't know how. When I tried to tell the other kids, they all laughed at me.

"Be quiet, Alexia," said Wrigley Davis, the second meanest boy at school. "He's not a bear. He's a funny, silly man in a costume."

"That's right," said Nolie McGowan, another mean kid. "Go eat a worm, Alexia."

It was obvious that I was on my own. I knew that I had to outsmart the bear. He was certainly a clever bear, so I would have to be just a tiny bit *more* clever than him.

I was ready for the challenge.

When the magic show was over, the Birthday Bear asked Mrs. McNatt if he could use the bathroom. This was all part of his sneaky plan.

"Of course you may!" Mrs. McNatt said with a huge smile. She thought nothing of it. "You're such a wonderful entertainer. You may use our bathroom anytime."

"Thank you," the Birthday Bear said. "I'll be right back, kids!"

While the Birthday Bear was inside the house, Mrs. McNatt passed Melvin his birthday presents one at a time.

Melvin didn't even bother reading any of the cards. He tore the wrapping off his gifts and tossed the cards onto the ground. But to my surprise, Melvin liked my gift the best.

"Who is it from?" asked Mrs. McNatt.

"I dunno," Melvin said.

I raised my hand. "The basketball was my gift to Melvin."

"And what do we say, Melvin?" said Mr. McNatt.

"Thank you, Alexia," Melvin said in his robot voice.

"That's a good boy," said Mr. McNatt. "Now, who would like to—"

Brrrrr-ring!

His cell phone rang.

"Be right back!" Mr. McNatt said as he stepped away to answer the call.

A moment later, he came back and explained that one of his patients had come down with a terrible case of foot fungus, so he had to leave the party and go to his office.

Nobody cared because they were too busy stuffing themselves with sweets or playing with the magic stuff that the Birthday Bear left lying on the table.

"Be back in one hour, kids!" Mr. McNatt said. Then he dashed out the gate on the right side of the house. I heard his car start up, followed by the sound of squealing tires.

"Okay, kids," said Mrs. McNatt, standing

up and taking charge. She was now the host of the party. "Which of you would like to—"

Brrrrr-ring!

Her cell phone rang.

Mrs. McNatt stepped away to answer her phone. She came back a moment later and explained that one of her patients had come down with a terrible toothache. She also had to leave the party and go to her office.

Melvin and his friends paid no attention.

"Be back in one hour, kids!" Mrs. McNatt said. Then off she went, dashing through the backyard and out the gate on the left side.

I heard another car start up, followed by the sound of more squealing tires.

As soon as the McNatts were both gone, the Birthday Bear returned.

"Oh no!" said the Birthday Bear, pretending to look surprised. "It looks like all the adults suddenly had to leave. And it looks like the nanny decided to have a little nap over by the pool."

We all turned and saw that the Birthday Bear wasn't lying. Our only adult supervision was asleep in a lawn chair, snoring away.

"I guess we can have fun by ourselves," the Birthday Bear said. "What do you say, kids? Can we have loads of fun without any adults to get in the way?"

Everyone cheered.

Not me.

I knew the situation was grim. We were being led on by a nasty old bear that wanted to eat us all for lunch. I had to come up with a plan, *fast*.

Chapter 8

The Most Amazing Trick of All

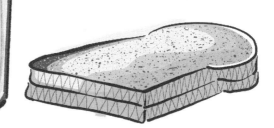

Well, kids? How about another magic trick?" the Birthday Bear said. "I have one more to show you all. And this one I think you will really like."

The kids all clapped and cheered.

"Show us another magic trick!" Melvin shouted. Then all his friends shouted too.

"Magic! Magic!" everyone cheered.

I couldn't believe that no one else had spotted this phony. The Birthday Bear licked his lips every time he looked at us. His eyes got big too, as if he wasn't even looking at a group of kids at all, but staring at a huge feast.

I was the only one who didn't fall for the Birthday Bear's charm. I knew that he wanted nothing more than to stick us between two huge slices of bread, chew us up, and then wash us down with a nice cold glass of milk.

The whole thing was a trap.

"Who wants birthday cake?" the Birthday Bear asked. "Who wants a huge slice of Melvin's delicious birthday cake, smothered with ice cream?"

Everyone did.

"Okay then," the Birthday Bear said. "Everyone inside the house! We'll have some cake, and then I'll show you my final magic trick. And I promise it will be the most amazing trick of all."

All the kids raced across the lawn, with Melvin leading the way. The back door slid open, and everyone ran inside the house.

I stayed behind.

I wanted to confront the bear and tell him that I knew all about his awful plan. I didn't know what his exact plan was…but I knew it involved eating ten delicious kids.

Once we were alone, I stood up to him. With my arms crossed, I looked way up into his dark brown eyes.

"I know what you're up to, you mean old nasty bear," I told him. "I know that you plan to eat us all up, one by one. You might have fooled everyone else, but you don't fool me. I know it's a trick."

"Trick?" said the Birthday Bear. He tried to act innocent. "What trick?"

"It was *you* who made those phone calls," I said. "You went inside the house pretending that you needed to use the bathroom. But you didn't need to use the bathroom. You needed to hide, so you could make a phony phone call."

"Who? Me?" the Birthday Bear said. "Why would I do such a thing?"

"To get rid of the adults," I said, as if his own horrible plan needed to be explained to him. "You went inside and probably used Melvin's cell phone to call Mr. and Mrs. McNatt. Then you probably used star-sixty-seven to block the number, so they wouldn't know it was you calling."

The Birthday Bear looked shocked.

"Then you disguised your voice and

made up a story about a fake emergency," I went on. "After Mr. McNatt left, you did the same thing to Mrs. McNatt. That's how you tricked the grownups into leaving."

The Birthday Bear sniffed. "What about the nanny?" he asked. "She would have seen me or tried to stop me."

"I'm not exactly sure what you did to the nanny," I admitted. "My guess is that you put some kind of sleeping medicine in her iced tea. Or maybe she fainted after she discovered that you're a *real* bear."

The Birthday Bear's cold brown eyes glared down at me. He sure didn't like the fact that I'd discovered his tricks.

"ROOAAAAAR!" growled the Birthday Bear, then he chased me inside the house.

Chapter 9

Caught by the Birthday Bear

The party guests sat around the dining room table, chanting and banging their silverware on the table.

"We–want–cake!"

"We–want–cake!"

"Bring–us–the–cake!"

The Birthday Bear was in the kitchen,

lighting candles for the cake. The lights were dimmed, then he came into the dining room carrying a big cake with a bunch of glowing candles on top.

Everyone sang the birthday song.

"Happy birthday to you!"

"Happy birthday to you!"

"Happy birthday, dear Melvin…"

While all the other kids were singing, I took the opportunity to sneak away.

I went to call my parents.

I planned to tell them that a great big bear was on the loose, and they needed to come rescue us right away.

I made it out of the dining room without being noticed. Melvin's cell phone was in the bathroom, right where the Birthday Bear left it. So I grabbed it and crept downstairs as quickly (and quietly) as I could.

The bear had no idea what I was up to. I decided he was a dumb bear, and that he deserved to be caught and placed in a zoo.

I began to dial my dad's number.

When I was feeling pretty good about my plan, and being so clever, I heard the noises.

Squeak.

Squeak.

Squeak.

Something big was coming downstairs.

First I saw a wet, black nose.

Then a mouth full of sharp teeth.

Then cold brown eyes, staring at me.

I was caught.

"What are you doing down here, little girl?" the Birthday Bear asked me. "You weren't calling your parents, were you?"

My legs felt wobbly.

My knees began to shake.

"I, um…" I couldn't think of anything clever to say, so I lied. "Of course not," I told the bear. "I wasn't calling my mom and dad."

"You're a liar!" shouted the Birthday Bear. He came all the way into the basement. The closer he got, the meaner his eyes became. He got so close that I could feel his hot breath on my face. He backed me into a corner. I thought he was going to eat me right then.

"You wouldn't deny me a nice hot meal, would you?" the Birthday Bear asked. "I just woke up from a long winter's nap and I'm really hungry."

I had to be brave.

"You must be starving after such a long cold winter," I said, trying to sound sincere.

I'm pretty good at telling fibs. Being able to tell a decent fib is not something I'm proud of, but it comes in handy sometimes.

"If you ate only *nine* children," I went on, "you would probably still be hungry."

"Correct, little girl. Ten is the perfect amount. I will be perfectly full if I eat ten children."

"Should we go back upstairs then, Mr. Bear?" I asked. "If you let us eat birthday cake and ice cream first, then we will all be plump and juicy. You will be so full after eating us that you'll need to lie down and take a nap."

The Birthday Bear thought it over. He looked at me with those mean, brown eyes. He was trying to make sure that I wasn't trying to trick him. I could tell that this bear was not entirely dumb. He was testing me to see if I was telling the truth.

"Okay, I suppose we have a deal," the Birthday Bear said. Then he pointed to the stairs with his snout. "Ladies first."

I had no choice but to go back upstairs and join the other kids. We were all going to sit around the table and enjoy our last slice of birthday cake. Then we would all be eaten up by a mean old nasty bear.

I was running out of time.

We were *all* running out of time.

I had to save them.

Chapter 10

Don't Tell Lies

Thank goodness Melvin brought his new favorite present with him into the house. He hadn't put it down since he tore open the package. It sat in his lap the whole time, even while stuffing his face.

When everyone had finished their cake and ice cream, the Birthday Bear prepared to show us his final trick.

All the kids from school just sat there smiling, with cake crumbs and ice cream smeared all over their faces. They still didn't realize what was about to happen. Not even when the Birthday Bear took off his silly hat, silly red nose, and tied a bib around his neck.

I raised my hand.

"I'll bet you can't balance Melvin's basketball on your nose," I said to the bear.

The Birthday Bear could feel the eyes of all the other kids watching him, and waiting for a response. They also wanted to see if this could be done.

"Of course I can," the Birthday Bear said, laughing off my challenge. "I'll prove it right now." Then he grabbed the ball from Melvin's hands. "I can balance this basketball on the end of my nose as simple as one, two, three."

"To the count of one hundred?" I asked.

It wouldn't be much time, but I thought that counting to a hundred would give me enough time to explain to everyone what was about to happen.

The Birthday Bear lifted the basketball up and placed it on his nose. It remained there, perfectly balanced. He stuck his hairy arms out to the side to help him keep still. His eyes were going cross-eyed from staring at the ball on the end of his nose.

"See?" the Birthday Bear said. "What did I tell you? Now I need one of you to count backwards from one hundred. And just as soon as we get to zero, I will show you my most incredible trick. You are all going to love it, I promise."

Because he was the birthday boy, Melvin got to do the counting. He was really terrible at it. I didn't know if he was kidding or not.

"One hundred, ninety-nine…" Melvin counted. "Ninety-six, ninety-five, uh, ninety-something…"

I began to explain to everyone what was really going on. I tried to tell them we were all going to be in serious trouble just as soon as Melvin finished counting backwards.

They all laughed and teased me when I tried to tell them the Birthday Bear was just a few seconds away from revealing that he was a real bear.

"Be quiet, Alexia," said Wrigley Davis, then he stuck his tongue out at me. "He is not a real bear. He's only dressed up like a bear. You're such a weirdo, *Alex*."

"Yes, he is!" I told them. "He's a *real* bear with *real* claws, and *real* sharp teeth that are going to chew you up like…like a…" I was so frustrated that I could hardly speak properly.

"Chew us up like what, Alexia?" said another mean kid. "Gummy bears?"

"Yes! Exactly like that," I whispered.

No one listened to me. They were having too much fun cheering on the Birthday Bear.

"You have to trust me!" I told them, but it was useless. No one believed me.

Time was running out.

"What's the count?" the Birthday Bear asked. "How much longer do I need to balance this ball on the end of my nose?"

"Forty-five more seconds, Mr. Bear," Melvin said. "Forty-four, forty-three…um, forty…"

I didn't know if Melvin was counting wrong on purpose or if he really had that much trouble counting backwards.

Again and again, I tried to warn the other kids about what was going to happen.

"Quit telling lies, Alexia," said one kid. "You're making the whole thing up. I want to see if he really can balance that basketball on his nose for a hundred count."

"Me too," said Wrigley Davis. "Once I saw a seal do the same trick at the zoo. But that was with a beach ball, and it only lasted a few seconds."

"I'm not kidding!" I said.

"Oh, zip your lip, Alex," said Katrina Belcher, the only other girl at the party. She had chocolate frosting smeared on her cheeks, and a mean scowl on her face.

"Don't listen to her," Katrina said to everyone at the table. "Alexia is dumb, spelled capital D-U-M."

"I'm not dumb. I'm telling the truth," I said. Not only was Katrina Belcher the meanest girl I knew, she was also a bad speller.

I tried again.

"You all have to escape! There isn't a person inside that costume. He's a great big bear, and he is going to eat us for lunch."

Katrina made a face at me.

Melvin had already started counting backwards from ten. I only had a few seconds left to think of something.

I had no choice.

I made up another fib.

Chapter 11

Free Money!

"The bank is handing out free money today," I told everyone. It was tough to keep a straight face. "But you have to be there before two o'clock."

The time was now 1:45 p.m.

"There's just enough time for you to get down to the bank," I said. "But only if you hurry up and leave right now."

Every kid knows that birthday parties are excellent fun. But free money is something no one can resist.

"Free money?"

S-S-S-S-WHOOSH!

Eight kids rushed for the front door.

My classmates had all been tricked by me, but it was for their own good. Now there were only two of us left.

Me and Melvin.

The front door slammed shut just as Melvin finished counting backwards from one hundred.

"Zero!" Melvin said. "You did it, Mr. Bear. I knew you could do it! You're the best!"

The great big bear let the basketball roll off the end of his nose. Then he stood up to his full, terrifying height. His huge body grew, and grew, and grew until his head bumped against the eight-foot-tall ceiling. His squinty brown eyes were now red, fierce, hungry eyes. Gobs of drool dripped down off his stained, pointy teeth.

Melvin's face suddenly turned very pale. He looked at me, and I looked at him. We were both terrified beyond words.

I was right.

The Birthday Bear was an **IMPOSTER**.

Melvin and I were both so scared that we didn't know what to do. Good thing that one of us can concentrate under pressure.

The bear looked around the table, wondering where everybody went. Then he glared at us. He was mad now that eight of the kids he planned on eating had escaped. Now there were only two kids left, which would leave him hungry for more.

"ROOOOAR!" growled the bear.

Melvin screamed so loud it hurt my ears.

The nasty old bear chased us around the dining room, the living room, and finally into the kitchen. The kitchen led right out onto the patio, and into the backyard.

Soon we were back where we started.

"Run, Melvin!" I yelled.

"I am running!" Melvin yelled back. "I'm too full of cake and ice cream!"

Melvin and I dodged left, then right, avoiding the bear as best we could. We ran from one end of the backyard to the other, then all the way back again.

"Stop running!" shouted the bear. He swiped at us with his huge hairy paws. "Stop running so I can catch you and eat you! Those foolish parents will be back soon!"

We were trapped.

Melvin and I were on one side of the

party table, with the bear on the other side. All he had to do was shove the table out of the way, then reach out and grab us.

"You really are an annoying brat," the bear said, looking right at me. "I'm going to enjoy eating *you* the most. I'll eat that one—" He pointed at Melvin. "—in two huge bites. But *you*..." He licked his lips. "I'm going to take my time eating you, crunching each bone, one by one."

I'd never been so scared in all my life. I couldn't imagine what it was going to feel like being lunch for a hungry bear.

It was a good thing that I knew all about bears. I learned from reading books that bears never back down from a challenge.

So I challenged him to a contest.

"Wait!" I shouted. "Don't eat us just yet."

"Why not?" the bear asked. He was upset

because he was getting hungrier by the minute. He couldn't wait any longer.

"We should have a contest," I told him. "To prove that you, ah…"

"Yes?"

"To prove who is smarter," I said. "You or me." Standing there on the other side of the table, being glared at by a hungry bear, my only thought was to run away as fast as I could.

Melvin wasn't a fast runner, so I knew he'd be gobbled up in two seconds. And besides, I wasn't going to let a dumb old bear get the best of me. I would show him who was smarter.

"A contest, huh?" the bear said, scratching his chin. "What kind of contest?"

"How about a riddle contest?" I said.

After thinking about it, the bear agreed.

"A battle of the brains?" he asked me.

I nodded. "Yes, exactly."

"Best two out of three?" he asked.

"Agreed," I said.

Everyone sat down at the table.

The **Battle of the Brains** was about to begin.

Chapter 12

Battle of the Brains

The bear and I stared each other down. I knew I had to bring my A-game, or else Melvin and I would find ourselves inside the bear's huge tummy.

"You go first," I suggested.

"I don't think so," the bear said. "I am bigger, so *I* will go first."

"That's what I just said," I told him. I knew this wasn't going to be much of a brain battle.

The bear looked embarrassed.

"Oh. Right," he said. Then he leaned back so far that the legs of the chair creaked under all his weight. His big belly stuck up over the table. He rubbed one huge, hairy paw on his chin while he thought about how to start.

"Let's see…" said the bear. Then he kept thinking while scratching his hairy forehead.

Finally, he gave me his first riddle.

"If a tree falls in the forest and it makes a sound…does anyone care?"

I answered, "No."

"Rrrrrr…" The bear growled and slammed his paw on the table. "Okay, I'll give you that one." With a grunt, he added, "Your turn. And it better not be a tricky one."

I gave him a funny look. "It's a riddle contest. Riddles are supposed to be tricky. That's the whole point of a riddle."

The bear rolled his eyes. "Whatever. I'm still going to win."

I thought about all the riddles I knew, but I was worried that the bear might know them too. So I made up my own riddle.

"Who pulls and pulls with all his might, but he's so shy he only comes out at night?"

I wish I had a cell phone like Melvin, so I could have taken a picture of the bear's face. He couldn't have looked more stunned if I took a fresh squiggly salmon and smacked him across the face with it.

"That's not fair!" cried the bear. "I don't know that one."

"Of course you don't know that one," I said. "I just made it up. What's the answer?"

The bear nervously chewed on his sharp claws. He thought about the riddle for so long that I knew he was stalling.

"Well?" I asked him.

"Just give me another minute," growled the bear. "I'm still thinking."

Melvin sat there the whole time, doing nothing. He seemed to have forgotten that we were going to be eaten, so he started nibbling on some of the leftover food.

I glared at him, so he put down his plastic fork and stopped goofing around.

"Sorry," Melvin said. "I'll pay attention."

The bear was completely at a loss for words. He was groaning and fidgeting, looking all around, searching for some sort of clue.

Unfortunately, when he looked up…

The answer was right there in the sky.

"The moon!" cried the bear. He pointed one huge paw up at the sleeping moon, which was still perfectly visible in the daytime.

"The moon pulls with gravity," said the bear. "And it only comes out at night. That's the answer to the riddle!"

Melvin made an irritated noise.

"Way to go, Alexia," he said. "He figured that one out easy."

I threw a plastic spoon at him. "Then why don't you come up with a riddle, Melvin?"

"No way! I don't know any riddles," Melvin said. "You do it. But if you lose and we get eaten, I'm telling everyone it was *your* fault."

A look came across the bear's hairy face, and I knew that he had finally come up with his second riddle.

The bear leaned in close.

"If a train goes from Wichita to the west coast traveling one hundred miles per hour, covering a distance of 1200 miles…"

The bear grinned at me.

"And another train leaves Wichita going to the east coast traveling at one hundred and ten miles per hour, covering a distance of 1300 miles...which one will reach the coast first?"

I had to think for a moment.

But soon I had the answer.

"There are no trains that leave Wichita," I said. "They have a few buses, but no passenger trains. You would have to travel to Topeka, the state capital, to find a passenger train."

His mouth fell open, revealing all his ugly teeth. "How did—? How do you—?"

After a huge sigh, the bear said, "How come you know all this stuff?"

"Simple," I told him. "Kids like Melvin don't read books and learn things. They play video games all day long, and pick on smart kids like me. I read books and research stuff on the Internet."

With his head buried in his huge paws, the bear started groaning. After he got a hold of himself, he looked up at me with a pitiful look on his face.

"Best four out of seven?"

"You said best two out of three!" I shouted.

Normally I don't get that mad. But this bear had lied to us, threatened to eat us, and now he was changing the rules just because he lost. I knew he wouldn't play fair.

"Fine," I told him. "Best four out of seven."

Before I could ask my next riddle, the bear stole my turn.

"I've got it!" The bear smacked his huge paw on the table. "You will never guess this one in a million years. Here it is…"

The bear cleared his throat.

"How much wood could a woodchuck chuck if a woodchuck could chuck wood?"

The bear looked very proud of himself.

I couldn't believe he thought he could fool me with such an outdated riddle. This one was easy. Especially since I had just read something about this very subject.

"I read an article online recently about woodchucks," I told him. "A bunch of bored scientists actually tried to prove that very question. Instead of using the word 'chuck' to mean actually throwing wood, they argued that it meant to eat wood. A woodchuck's stomach *can* digest wood, but it's not their favorite food. They like to eat grass and bugs. So I guess the whole experiment was pointless. Woodchucks don't eat wood, or chuck it. They've got better things to do."

The bear was stunned.

Now it was my turn to ask a riddle.

I made one up on the spot.

"What is round without a middle," I said. "Jumps high, but has no legs?"

"Oh no," the bear groaned. "Not another tricky one."

While he sat there thinking and scratching his head, Melvin practically gave him the answer. Sitting there quietly during the brain battle between me and the bear, Melvin got bored. He began to practice twirling his basketball on the end of his finger like the professional players. He was terrible at it. But he made enough of a distraction that the bear looked at him and found the clue.

"A ball!" the bear said. "A ball is round and has no middle. It has only air in the middle. And when you bounce it, a ball can jump very high, even without legs!"

"Okay, you got that one," I said. "But only because Melvin helped you."

The bear had his next riddle.

"What is the proper meaning of the phrase...*Does a bear poop in the woods*?"

The bear leaned back in his chair with a big grin on his face. I guess he thought he would win with that one.

"That phrase has no meaning," I told him. "What you just said...is an idiom."

The bear sat up and growled at me. "What did you just call me?"

"*Idiom*," I repeated. "It's a way of speaking. That phrase doesn't require an answer because it doesn't need one. People go to the bathroom in a house because that's where they live. Bears go to the bathroom in the woods because that's where they live."

"Actually, we bears prefer to go in a cave,"

the bear explained. "Even bears need a little privacy. But you are correct, little girl. That phrase is one of those *idiom* things."

"Okay, so then I won."

"Huh? No you didn't," the bear said. "I said best out of seven."

"I know," I told him. "You guessed only two of my riddles, but I've already guessed four of your lame riddles. I win."

Counting on his paws, the bear realized I wasn't lying. I had won. But that didn't stop him from changing the rules again. "Let's go best six out of ten, okay?"

"You said best four out of seven!" I yelled.

"Well, I changed my mind," the bear said. "Best six of ten."

"No."

"Best eleven out of twenty?"

"No."

"Best fifty-one out of a hundred?" The bear could tell by the furious look I was giving him that he wasn't going to win this argument.

"Okay, if you can answer one more question," the bear said, "then I will let you both go."

"Just one question?" I asked, watching him carefully. "And if I answer it correctly, then you'll leave? Just go right back out the way you came in?"

"Yep. I promise."

"Deal," I said.

The bear leaned in close and narrowed his brown eyes, which were kind of bloodshot and scary. Then he asked me the most impossible question ever.

"When is *my* birthday?" asked the bear with a big smirk on his hairy face.

I glared at him with my arms folded. "That's not a fair question."

The bear laughed. "It's a battle of the brains! I can ask you anything I want. Now, answer the question or I'm going to eat you and your little friend."

Before I could answer, Melvin ruined it.

"September fifteenth?" Melvin guessed.

"Melvin!" I shouted. "What are you doing?"

"Ha! Wrong answer!" The bear laughed and pointed at us. Then he got up and started doing a little happy dance.

"My birthday is on September sixteenth!" cheered the bear. "You lose, I win! Now I get to eat you both for lunch!"

Melvin and I were shocked as we watched the bear rise up to his full height. He was by far the biggest bear I'd ever seen.

He was huge!

"And now..." the bear said. "It's *my* turn for lunch."

Melvin and I did the only thing we could do at a time like this.

We ran.

Chapter 13

The Biggest Splash Contest

Melvin and I were soon out of breath from running so much. Too bad for us that the bear wasn't breathing heavy at all. He was so big and strong that he would eventually catch us.

"Stop running from me!" roared the bear. "All this running is making me hungry. Now get over here, both of you!"

The nanny was still asleep by the pool,

snoring away. She was probably having a dream about making a phone call. She had her pinky finger pressed to her lips, her thumb pressed against her ear, and she was mumbling in her sleep.

This gave me an idea.

I tried to explain my plan to Melvin as we ran all over the backyard, dodging the bear at every turn.

"Meet me over by the pool!" I shouted to Melvin. "I have an idea!"

"What? Where? Why?" Melvin was scared and really out of breath. Thankfully, he did what I told him without asking any more dumb questions. He certainly wasn't going to come up with a plan to stop the bear from chomping us, so it was all up to me.

Good thing I can work under pressure.

"ROOOOOAR!"

The bear had us cornered over by the pool. "Ha-ha! Now I've got you! Get over here!"

We couldn't climb over the fence because it was so tall. And also because the thick shrubs, thorny roses, and prickle bushes blocked that escape route. There was nowhere left for us to run.

"No escaping now," the bear said as he closed in on me and Melvin.

I pointed to the swimming pool. "I bet you that I can make a bigger splash than you. I may be smaller than you, but I'll bet I can do it."

"Is that so?" the bear said with a sniff.

"Yes it is," I told him, keeping my cool. "And so can Melvin. We're going to prove it to you right now. We'll have one last contest. A splashing contest. If neither one of us can make a bigger splash than you, then you can eat us both for lunch. No more running, no more tricks. A bet is a bet."

"You promise you'll stop running?" the bear asked. "You'll stand still and let me eat you up? Bite by bite?"

"I promise," Melvin said. He was still huffing and puffing from all the running. "No more running. I can't…run…anymore."

"I promise too," I told him. Then without another word, I took a running jump into the shallow end of the pool, clothes and all. Water splashed up into the air, but not very high.

"Not bad," the bear said. "Not bad at all for such a tiny little girl."

"My turn!" Melvin said. He took a running jump, tucked his knees up to his chest, and splashed into the pool beside me.

Sploosh!

Melvin's splash was nearly twice as high as mine. But I knew it still wasn't good enough to win. But that was part of my plan.

"Not bad, not bad." The bear actually applauded Melvin. "But now it's my turn," he said, heading for the deep end.

The bear took one, two, three big bounces off the diving board.

"Geronimo!" he shouted. Then he came down with a tremendous *smack!* on top of the water. His splash was more than twice as high as Melvin's. There was no sense in trying to argue about who's splash was bigger.

The bear had clearly won.

Lucky for us, the whole thing was a trick.

"Get out of the pool and run," I whispered to Melvin. "Run as fast as you can. Don't look back."

Before the bear knew what was happening, Melvin and I were out of the pool and running across the backyard. I headed one way and Melvin the other.

The bear had no idea that he had been tricked. He was just happy that he had won the contest.

"I won! I won!" the bear cheered, splashing around in the deep end of the pool. "Now I get to gobble you up! Ha-Ha! I'm the most clever bear there ever was!"

Suddenly, his cheering turned into screaming. He started to panic.

"HELP!" cried the bear. "I can't swim! I'm going to drown! Help me!"

Melvin and I made it to the gates, him on the right and me on the left. I stopped, but Melvin kept on going. He didn't stop running until he was way down at the end of the street. And even then he didn't stop. He was probably on his way down to the bank to see if he could still get any of the "free money" I had told everyone about earlier.

"Help!" the bear screamed. "I'm going to drown if you don't help me! Won't you please help me, little girl? What did I ever do to you?"

I felt bad for the bear. He was very clever at magic tricks, but he wasn't very bright when it came to other stuff. If he had just read even one book about bears, or asked some of his bear friends, he would have known that bears are excellent swimmers.

"Bears can swim just fine," I called to him. "I've seen them do it at the zoo, which is where you belong."

"We can?" the bear asked. "Are you sure?" He was trying to climb out, but he was so big and huge that his claws just scraped and scraped on the edge of the pool. It never occurred to him to swim toward the shallow end and use the ladder.

"Yes, I am sure that bears can swim," I told him. "Just kick your legs and flap your arms. You'll figure it out!"

The bear kicked his legs, flapped his arms, and began to swim.

"Hey, look at me! I'm swimming like a pro!" The bear was so happy about his swimming skills that he completely forgot about how hungry he was. He enjoyed swimming so much that he stayed in the deep end until he taught himself how to do the backstroke.

And that's how he got caught.

Because I ran home and called the zoo.

P.S.

In the end, it was me who saved my classmates from the Birthday Bear that day, not Melvin. But that's what he told everyone. That *he* tricked the bear and saved us.

It doesn't bother me.

At least he doesn't try to make me eat worms at school anymore. Once he even invited me over to his house on a Saturday morning to play basketball.

"Maybe later," I told him. "Today I'm going to the zoo with my dad. I have a special homework assignment about bears."

Melvin ran away screaming. "No more bears! I can't tell which ones are fake and which ones are real! I never want to see another bear as long as I live!"

And that is exactly the reason why I wrote this down. So that you don't fall for the same trick. I made up a list of things to watch out for if you ever get invited to a birthday party with a special guest.

What to watch out for:

Long pointy teeth
Terrible breath
Lip-smacking
Hairy back
Small, floppy ears
No zipper

I hope this list helps. Sometimes it's hard to spot an **IMPOSTER**. I would do it for you, but I can't be at all your birthday parties, now can I?

Good luck!

Alexia

Discussion Questions:

Bullying is a big part of this story. Melvin McNatt is an obvious bully. Can you name any other bullies from the story? Why do you think they are bullies?

What are some different ways that Alexia challenged her bullies?

Do you think Alexia made good decisions when handling bullies? Why or why not?

Do you think Alexia is a bully? Why or why not?

Have you ever met a bully? What did you do?

What are some ways to stop a bully?

Bullying Resources*

Pacer Center Kids Against Bullying
http://www.pacerkidsagainstbullying.org

Stop Bullying
http://www.stopbullying.gov

Stomp Out Bullying
https://www.stompoutbullying.org/

Thank you for purchasing and reading *Alexia & Melvin: The Birthday Bear*.

Handersen Publishing is an independent publishing house that specializes in creating quality young adult, middle grade, and picture books.

We hope you enjoyed this book and will consider leaving a review on Amazon or Goodreads. A small review can make a big difference.

Thank you.

Keep reading to find out what happens next!

That mean old bear is back! Can Alexia and Melvin spot an imposter…again?

Chapter 1

How Melvin and I Became Friends

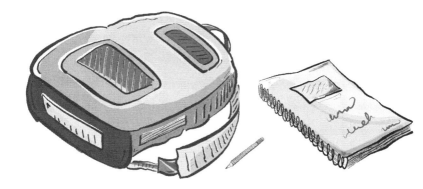

Ever since I saved Melvin from that mean old bear, we've been hanging out together. We play at his house all the time now. And he comes over to my house for dinner at least a couple times a week.

Melvin was a bully.

Now he's my friend.

I help him with science, math, English, social studies, and pretty much every single subject in school. And Melvin teaches me all the stuff he knows, like basketball, skateboarding, drawing comic books, and playing video games.

Those aren't really the types of things I'm into, but it's still fun to hang out. Otherwise I would probably stay at home and read books all day, or research stuff on the Internet.

Sometimes Melvin and I joke about running into that bear again. A mean, nasty bear that called himself the Birthday Bear.

I used my brain to outsmart him. That's another reason why Melvin likes to hang out with me—for protection, I guess.

Sometimes you can't out-muscle a bully.

Sometimes a bully has to be outsmarted.

Melvin and I could forget about bullies for now because school was done for the week. We had a glorious Saturday and Sunday ahead of us.

"My house first?" Melvin asked. "We can play a little one-on-one? Or play one of my new video games?"

"Homework first," I told him as we walked over to his house. "Then basketball."

"Oh," Melvin said with a smirk. "I forgot."

After school on Fridays, I always help Melvin with his homework. After that, we play at his house for a while, then go have dinner at my house. Since Melvin and I have become such good friends, we're usually inseparable on Saturday and Sunday.

Weekends are great, but we also had something fun to look forward to at school on Monday. Our class was going on a field trip to the Natural History Museum.

Melvin and I were both excited.

I had no idea that our field trip to the museum would turn out to be the *second* worst day of my life.

The worst day of my life was the day I met that mean old nasty bear.

Same goes for Melvin.

Miserable Melvin

On our field trip to the Natural History Museum, Melvin sat beside me on the bus. The bus ride was bumpy because of the bumpy road, and the bumpy seats.

Mostly it was lumpy.

Chunky, too.

That's because of the lumpy chunks of peanut butter sandwich that some bullies were throwing at us.

Actually, they were aiming for Melvin.

Not *me* for a change.

"Nice friends," I said to Melvin as he picked a hunk of peanut butter goo off the back of his shirt.

"They're not my friends," Melvin said. "Well, not anymore."

Wrigley Davis, Nolie McGowan, and the rest of Melvin's old group of bullies were all sitting a few rows behind us on the bus.

"Hungry, Melvin?" said Wrigley Davis. "Have a bite of this nummy sandwich!"

Splat!

Wrigley Davis was the new leader. He was trying to prove to everyone that he was going to be the best bully in the history of bullies. I guess he was trying to be an even better bully than Melvin *used* to be.

"Just ignore them," I told Melvin.

"Easy for you to say," Melvin said. "They're aiming for me, not—"

Splat!

"—you."

The peanut butter splat attack lasted for the entire bus ride. Wrigley Davis must have had the world's biggest sandwich in his backpack, because the attack seemed to go on forever.

"I should have worn a hat today," Melvin said quietly. Then he pulled off a chunky glob and flicked it onto the floor.

Melvin looked miserable.

You might think that I would be happy, or feel better somehow by watching an ex-bully (like Melvin) getting a taste of what it felt like to be teased and bullied.

It didn't help.

In fact, it made me feel worse.

So I put a stop to it.

"Mr. Rockman!" I shouted, waving my hand in the air. "Over here, Mr. Rockman! I have to tell you something!"

Melvin froze. His face got all weird and he started making strange "Z" noises at me.

"Zzzzt!" said Melvin. "Zzzzzt!"

"What?" I said to him.

"Alexia, zip it!" Melvin begged. "Please?" He was terrified that I was going to tell the teacher and make things worse.

I was up to the challenge.

"Yes, Miss...?" Mr. Rockman looked at me. Then he looked down at his clipboard, back at me, and back at his clipboard again.

"My name is Alexia, sir," I told him. "I'm in Miss Mandy's accelerated class."

Splat!

A chunk of soggy sandwich sailed by. It just barely missed me, but hit Melvin.

"What is it, Alexia?" said Mr. Rockman. "We're running a bit late, but I think we'll arrive at the museum right when it opens. I can't wait to see the gem and rock exhibits!"

Mr. Rockman had a sparkle in his eye. I'd heard about this teacher. He loved rocks and gems more than anything in the world.

I raised my hand again.

"Yes, Alexia?" said Mr. Rockman.

"Wrigley was too scared to tell you, sir, but…" I waited until everyone was listening.

"Tell me what?" said Mr. Rockman.

"Wrigley Davis has terrible OBS," I said nice and loud for everyone to hear.

Mr. Rockman stared at me. "OBS?"

"Overactive Bladder Syndrome," I said, making sure every kid on the bus heard me.

"Wrigley has to go to the bathroom *aaaall* the time," I went on. "He wants to make sure we're going to have lots of potty breaks once we get to the museum."

Every kid on the bus was laughing.

Wrigley Davis turned so red and got so embarrassed that he started to eat what was left of his giant peanut butter sandwich. He shoved food into his mouth so he didn't have to look at anybody.

Mr. Rockman sighed. "Yes, Wrigley, they have bathrooms at the museum. You will just have to hold it until we get there."

Everyone laughed louder.

I was sure Melvin and I would pay for it later, but at least Wrigley Davis knew how it felt to be teased. I could tell that the bully didn't like being bullied.

But would he ever stop bugging us?

Probably not.

"Thanks," Melvin said, once the laughter died down. He looked a little less sad.

"You're welcome," I said. Then he and I both giggled about it all the way to the museum. The best part was that the peanut butter splat attack finally stopped.

As soon as we arrived at the museum, Melvin

and I quickly figured out that sloppy chunks of peanut butter sandwich were the least of our problems.

Waiting for us at the museum was a much bigger problem. A great big hairy problem with claws, fur, and sharp teeth.

And a very big appetite.

About the Author

Tevin Hansen is the author or illustrator of more than 20 children's books, and is also a songwriter, musician, and Lincoln Arts Council teaching artist. Tevin's "Rock & Read" programs for schools, museums, festivals, and community events incorporate reading with original folk-rock songs that entertain all ages. You can watch music videos for his songs on his YouTube channel.

Discover more at:
www.tevinhansen.com

Or follow Tevin on Facebook, Instagram, YouTube, and Twitter.

Read all three Alexia & Melvin chapter books!

Alexia and Melvin have a complicated relationship. And that mean old bear doesn't make things any easier.

Discover the ocean with the Sea Serpent of Science.

What constellation will you find with the Alien of Astronomy?

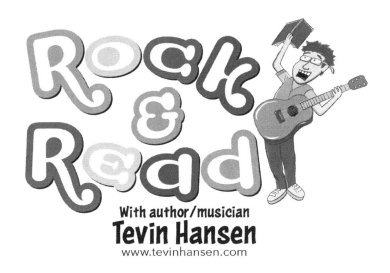

With author/musician
Tevin Hansen
www.tevinhansen.com

Schedule a visit for your school, library, or special
event with author/musician Tevin Hansen!

Original Music
Great Books
Author/Musician Events

Made in the USA
Middletown, DE
12 March 2022

62515654R00066